THE VILLAGE THAT ALMOST VANISHED

by
Steve Brezenoff

★

illustrated by
C.B. Canga

STONE ARCH BOOKS
www.stonearchbooks.com

Field Trip Mysteries are published by Stone Arch Books,
A Capstone Imprint
1710 Roe Crest Drive
North Mankato, Minnesota 56003
www.capstonepub.com

Library of Congress Cataloging-in-Publication Data
Brezenoff, Steven.
   The village that almost vanished / by Steve Brezenoff ;
illustrated by C.B. Canga.
       p. cm. — (Field trip mysteries)
   ISBN 978-1-4342-1611-3
   [1. School field trips—Fiction. 2. Mystery and detective
stories.]   I. Canga, C. B., ill. II. Title.
   PZ7.B7576Vi 2010
   [Fic]—dc22
       2009002575

Printed in the United States of America in Stevens Point, Wisconsin.
072013   007593R

                              Creative Director:
                                 Heather Kindseth
                              Graphic Designer:
                                 Carla Zetina-Yglesias

Summary:
Samantha Archer, also known as Sam, couldn't be
more excited about her class trip to Scrub Brush,
the cool frontier town. But from the second they
arrive at the historic village, it's clear someone's
trying to make the whole town disappear. Can Sam
and her friends save Scrub Brush?

★ TABLE OF CONTENTS ★

BIG BURGER

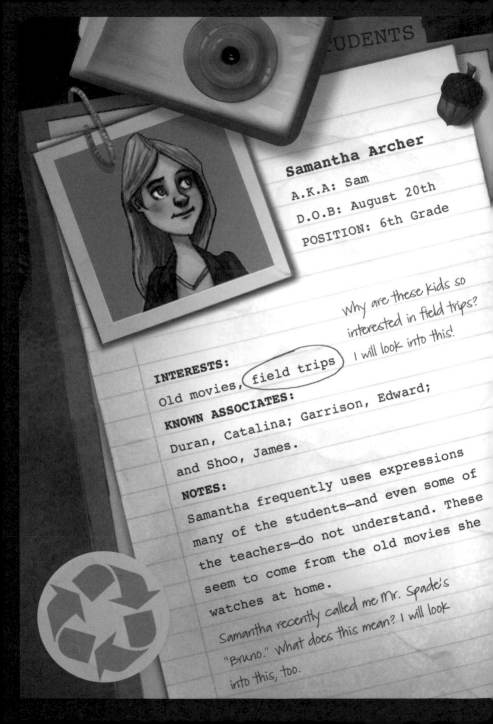

Samantha Archer

A.K.A: Sam

D.O.B: August 20th

POSITION: 6th Grade

Why are these kids so interested in field trips? I will look into this!

INTERESTS:
Old movies, field trips

KNOWN ASSOCIATES:
Duran, Catalina; Garrison, Edward; and Shoo, James.

NOTES:
Samantha frequently uses expressions many of the students—and even some of the teachers—do not understand. These seem to come from the old movies she watches at home.

Samantha recently called me Mr. Spade's "Bruno." What does this mean? I will look into this, too.

CHAPTER
ONE

I'm Samantha Archer.

You can call me Sam.

I'm twelve years old, five feet and eight inches tall, and I solve crimes with some help from my friends.

My friends and I have caught lots of crooks, usually when we go on field trips together. We all have our favorite tales about the cases we've solved, and this is mine.

It all started on a hot Friday morning. Egg and I were sitting on the curb in front of our school.

Egg's real name is Edward. His initials are E.G.G. That's why we call him Egg. He was fiddling with his camera, like always.

If you want to solve crimes, get a friend with a camera. Those pictures are great evidence.

Egg's duffel bag was next to him on the curb. We were both packed for a weekend away from home.

We were going on a field trip!

We go on lots of field trips at our school. They're usually pretty fun, and they're almost always exciting. But this field trip was the biggest of the year. Maybe the biggest of our whole lives.

This was the annual sixth-grade weekend trip to Scrub Brush. That's an old ghost town in the middle of nowhere.

Fifty years ago, some rich guy bought the whole empty town. He decided to turn the place into a living history lesson.

He brought in actors to play cowboys and saloon keepers and gold prospectors. Now, schools visit all the time.

We were really excited.

"Boy, it's hot today," Egg said.

"Yep," I said.

Just then, a shadow fell over me. I looked up and saw Anton Gutman.

"Hello, dorks," Anton said.

"Hello, Gutman," I replied. "Shouldn't you be getting into trouble someplace else?"

"Oh, I'll be getting into trouble," Anton said. He held up his overnight bag. "I have more tricks and practical jokes in this bag than you can imagine," he said with a chuckle.

"Mr. Spade will catch you," Egg said.

"Nah," Anton replied.

I shrugged. "Then we will," I said.

"Ooh, I'm so scared," Anton said. Then he walked away.

I looked down the street. "Here come Gum and Cat," I said.

Our friends were strolling like turtles down the sidewalk toward us. I couldn't blame them. It was pretty hot, and moving fast only made it feel hotter.

Finally they reached us. The four of us walked over to the bus.

The whole sixth grade was standing around Mr. Spade, our teacher. He looked at his watch. "Well, that's everyone," he said. "Let's go."

He got on the bus. All the kids piled on after him. The four of us sat in the back.

We were off on the most exciting field trip of our lives! Of course, we had no idea just how exciting it would be.

CHAPTER TWO

THE LONG ROAD

It's a long ride to Scrub Brush.

After an hour or so, the bus pulled off the road.

"Are we there?" Egg said.

"Can't be," I said. "We're only an hour from school. Scrub Brush is way farther than that."

Mr. Spade got up from his seat and faced the students. "Okay, everyone," he said. "We're going to take a break now."

I looked out the window. We were in front of a big gas station with a fast food place attached to it. A big sign read "BIG Stop." BIG Stop is a really popular fast food chain where we live. There are dozens of them.

"We'll get moving again in about twenty minutes," Mr. Spade said.

Cat and I went into the little restaurant. "I want to grab some fries," I said.

I ran to the counter and nearly knocked down an old man in a cowboy hat. He had been talking to a young woman in a business suit.

"Sorry," I said.

The man went back to talking to the young woman. I ordered some fries.

"I don't care what your offer is," the old man said. "I'm not selling my land to BIG Stop."

The woman sighed. She seemed upset. "If you change your mind, you know how to find me," she said. "Mr. G. won't be happy about this."

The old man didn't say anything. He just walked off.

I watched the woman. Suddenly she faced me.

"What do you want?"

she snapped.

I must have jumped about thirty feet. "Um, nothing," I stammered.

I forgot about my fries and headed for the door. Cat was waiting for me with Egg and Gum.

Mr. Spade was standing by the door of the bus as we got back on.

"Everyone, take a ticket from me as you get back on the bus please," Mr. Spade said.

He handed me a big blue ticket. "What's this for?" I asked.

"That's your ticket to Scrub Brush," Mr. Spade said. "You need that to get in."

"How much longer is the drive?" Gum asked as he took his own ticket.

"About another hour," Mr. Spade replied.

Once everyone was on the bus, we got settled in for some more driving.

I stared out the window. My stomach was rumbling. I wished I hadn't forgotten about my fries.

TWO RIDERS

We'd been on the road for another hour when the brakes squealed and the bus stopped.

Mr. Spade got up from his seat. The driver shut off the bus and pulled open the door.

"Okay, everyone," Mr. Spade said. "We're here! Grab your bags!"

Gum stepped off the bus right before I did. "Whoa," he said.

As my foot hit the dry ground, I looked up the road. Through the reddish dust, I could see several old, small buildings. It seemed like no one had been there for a hundred years.

Mr. Spade scratched his head. "Hmm," he mumbled. "I thought someone would be here to meet us."

Suddenly we heard a quiet *clomp, clomp.*

I shielded my eyes and gazed up the road. Through the dust, I spotted two figures moving toward us.

"Look, over there!" I said, pointing. "I see two people riding horses, and they're coming this way!"

Egg tried to take a photo, but it was too dusty to get a good shot.

"Welcome to **Scrub Brush, kids,**" a rider called.

The two riders reached us. One was a man with a huge mustache and dark hair. The other was a young woman. Both had shiny star-shaped badges on their shirts, and they were both wearing cowboy hats.

They got off their horses.

"I'm Sheriff Grady. You can call me Sheriff Bob," the man said.

The woman pulled off her hat. "And I'm Deputy Curtin," she said. "You can call me Deputy Laurie."

"It's great to meet you," Mr. Spade said, shaking their hands. "You folks weren't here last year, were you?"

Mr. Spade had been the sixth-grade teacher for years. He would have known the sheriff and deputy if they'd been there before.

"Nope," Sheriff Bob said. "We both joined Scrub Brush's law enforcement this season. Deputy Laurie will collect your tickets. I need to get back to town."

The sheriff put one foot in his horse's stirrup and swung up onto the saddle. The horse galloped back to town. The sheriff seemed like he was in a big hurry.

"All right," Deputy Laurie said. "Give me your tickets." She frowned. I wondered if she was angry about something.

Cat and I handed her our tickets. Then we followed Mr. Spade and the rest of the class toward the town.

"What's her problem?" Cat whispered.

I shrugged and looked back over my shoulder. The deputy held the reins of her horse. She started walking slowly back to town.

A THIRD BUNKMATE

"Three beds," Gum said. He sat on one of the tiny beds in the room he was sharing with Egg.

Cat and I had already dropped off our stuff in our room. A third girl, Eliza, was also in our room. She was cool enough.

"I wonder who will be our third person,"

Egg said, claiming a bed near the window.

Cat sat down. She said, "If there's only one bed left, you will end up with someone who no one else wants to bunk with."

Egg nodded. "Someone who's a big pain," he added.

I sat up straight. "You don't mean . . . ," I said.

"Oh no," Gum added, falling back onto his bed.

CREEEEEAK! The room's door was loud as it swung open.

"Hey, dorks." It was Anton Gutman. He swaggered in and dropped his bag onto the third bed.

"Hi, Anton," Cat said, smiling. She always tries to be pleasant to Anton, even though he calls us dorks.

"You guys are in luck," Anton said. He opened his bag and started digging through it. "You get the famous Anton Gutman in your room with you."

Gum rolled his eyes. "We need to hurry up," he said. "We're supposed to meet Mr. Spade on Main Street in a few minutes."

"Okay," I said. "Let's get going."

Anton waved us off. "I'll meet you there later," he said. "I have some urgent business first."

Anton grabbed his bag of tricks and zipped out the door ahead of us.

"What a weirdo," Cat said, shaking her head.

The bunkhouses were at the far end of Main Street. Scrub Brush only had two streets, which crossed in the middle of town.

One was called Main Street. The other was called First Street. Mr. Spade had asked us to gather at the corner of Main and First after we'd unpacked.

"This place is great," Egg said. He took some pictures as we strolled down Main Street.

Egg clicked photos of the Saloon, the General Store, the Feed Store, the Jail, and the Sheriff's Office.

As we walked past the Sheriff's Office, we heard some yelling coming from inside.

"What's that shouting?" I asked.

"Sounds like the deputy," Cat said. "And the sheriff."

"They're having an argument," Gum added. "I wonder what they're shouting about."

We all listened, but we couldn't tell what they were saying.

By the time we reached Mr. Spade at the corner, everyone else was already there. Even Anton.

"What took you dorks so long?" Anton asked. Then he started laughing.

The sheriff and deputy walked up. "Okay, everyone," Mr. Spade said. "Sheriff Bob will tell you about today's activities."

"Howdy, kids," Sheriff Bob said. The deputy looked very angry. "I'm afraid before we start, I have some bad news."

"You can say that again," Deputy Laurie said under her breath.

The sheriff glared at her, then went on. "I'm afraid your trip to Scrub Brush might be the last weekend for this camp," he said.

Mr. Spade's eyes shot wide open. "The last weekend?" he asked. "Why?"

"The money from this month's ticket sales has been stolen," the sheriff replied. "If we can't find that money, the land will have to be sold!"

MORE CRIMES

"Can you believe this?" Gum said as the four of us walked down First Street to the first activity.

"I know," Cat said. "We might be the last sixth graders from our school to visit Scrub Brush."

"From any school!" Egg pointed out.

I shrugged. "Of course, we'll have to find the cash," I said.

"Of course," Gum agreed. He blew a big bubble. "But where do we start?"

I thought about it. We didn't have much to go on.

"All we know is that Deputy Laurie and Sheriff Bob had a big fight," I said.

"Don't forget Anton," Gum added.

"You always blame Anton," Egg said. "What makes you think he did it?"

"Are you kidding?" Gum replied. "He's Anton."

I nodded. "True," I said. "Plus, earlier he said he had some urgent business."

Cat nodded. "We'll find more clues," she said. "Don't worry."

We caught up to the rest of the class at the blacksmith. Just as we got there, Mr. Spade and Deputy Laurie were stepping onto the blacksmith shop's porch.

There was a loud crack and then a big boom. The porch collapsed!

"Ah!" Mr. Spade cried out as he fell. The deputy fell right on top of him. They got to their feet quickly.

"What happened?" the sheriff asked as he came running over.

"How should I know?" Deputy Laurie said. "One of the kids could have been hurt!"

Just then, someone poked me in the back. I spun around.

I was eye to eye with a short old man. He wore a ragged cowboy hat. He had a funny white mustache and big bushy eyebrows.

"That would be a **shame,** wouldn't it?" the old man said.

"Huh?" I asked. Cat turned around too.

"If one of you kids got hurt," the old man explained. "That would be a shame."

"Sam and Cat," Mr. Spade said. "Please pay attention. We're all going to begin the activity."

We both turned quickly. "Sorry, Mr. Spade," I said. "This old man was—"

But when I turned back, the old man was gone.

I shrugged and looked at Cat. She raised her eyebrows.

The activity was pretty cool. We got to watch the blacksmith make horseshoes and put them on a horse. Then we each got to make our own fire pokers. We all got to swing the blacksmith's hammer. Red sparks flew everywhere!

At the end, we got to keep the fire poker. I knew my grandma would love it. Our fireplace doesn't work, but she would love to have the fire poker for a decoration.

After the activity, Mr. Spade led us to the Saloon for lunch. As he opened the swing door, a bucket of red paint came crashing down. Mr. Spade was totally covered in paint.

"What is this?" Mr. Spade cried out. Shocked, he looked down at his shirt and pants.

The sheriff and deputy walked into the Saloon. "What happened?" Sheriff Bob asked.

"What's it look like?" Deputy Laurie said. "Some joke!"

The whole class was totally silent. Except Egg's camera, which was clicking like mad.

"This town sure isn't what it used to be," Mr. Spade muttered. "Falling porches and cans of paint lying around!"

Egg looked around and then whispered to me, "Not to mention the stolen money."

I signaled for Cat and Gum to lean in close. "Maybe," I said quietly to my friends, "someone really wants to shut down Scrub Brush."

CHAPTER SIX

AROUND THE FIRE

After lunch, we watched Deputy Laurie do a lasso demonstration. Sheriff Bob wasn't around for that.

It was still very hot, but as the day went on, it started to cool down. By supper, it was even getting kind of chilly.

"It can get cold here at night," Mr. Spade said. "We're much higher up than we were back home."

Sheriff Bob and Deputy Laurie got a big campfire started. Soon dinner was ready.

We all sat at picnic tables to eat our baked beans and hot dogs. Each group of bunkmates was supposed to sit together. That meant our table was me, Cat, and Eliza, and Gum, Egg, and Anton Gutman.

"This food is gross," Anton said. He crossed his arms when Mr. Spade set a plate in front of him. "I want a BIG Burger with cheese and bacon and hot peppers."

"Well, I guess you're out of luck," Gum replied.

"I also want a BIG Soda," Anton added.

"Anton," I said, "the nearest BIG Stop is over an hour away, remember?"

The sheriff strolled over to us. "You kids enjoying the grub?" he asked. He made a face, like the food didn't look so good to him either.

"It's awful!" Anton replied.

"Don't be rude," Egg said. He took a bite of his hot dog. "It's very good, Sheriff Bob."

The sheriff ignored Egg.

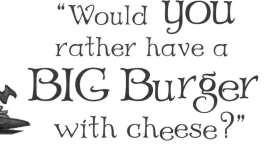

"Would **you** rather have a **BIG Burger** with cheese?"

Sheriff Bob asked Anton.

Anton smiled. "Yes, I would!" he replied.

The sheriff leaned down. "To tell you the truth, so would I," he said quietly. "I sure wish there was a BIG Stop near here. I'd take BIG Stop over this place any day!"

Anton nodded. "Me too," he said.

"My mom says BIG Stop food is super unhealthy," Cat said. "I'll stick with these beans."

Just then, Laurie came by. "Leave the kids alone, Bob," she said.

Then the sheriff and deputy walked away together, arguing quietly.

"That was weird," I said.

"Yeah," Egg agreed. "Sheriff Bob really loves BIG Stop."

"Hey, Egg," Cat said. "Let's see the pictures you've taken so far."

Anton shook his head. "That sounds boring," he said. Then he got up and walked off.

"Too bad for him," I said. "Show us those pictures, Egg."

Egg started clicking through the pictures. Soon he came to the ones he had taken at the blacksmith's.

"There's Mr. Spade right before he fell through the porch," Cat pointed out.

"Who's that?" I asked. I pointed to a figure in the background.

"I'm not sure," Gum said. "It kind of looks like Sheriff Bob."

Egg nodded. "The sheriff showed up right after the crash," he said.

"So why is he near the porch before it broke?" I asked. "That doesn't make sense."

Soon Egg came to the pictures of Mr. Spade covered in red paint. "Who else was at the Saloon?" I asked.

"I saw Deputy Laurie there," Cat said.

"I didn't see her," I told Cat.

Cat frowned. "I thought it was her. It was someone wearing a big hat. But she just snuck in and then left quickly."

I said, "Maybe she rigged the paint to fall on Mr. Spade."

"Why would she do that?" Cat asked.

"Who knows?" I said. "Why would Sheriff Bob rig the porch to collapse?"

"Maybe they're working together," Gum suggested.

"Those two?" I said. "No way. They're always fighting."

"Besides, the sheriff is in charge around here," said Egg. "Why would he want to start trouble? It's like, his job to stop trouble!"

"Don't be so sure,"
said a voice.

I spun around. The creepy old man from the blacksmith's shop was behind me.

"What do you mean?" Gum asked.

"Sheriff Bob Grady doesn't own Scrub Brush," the old man said.

He smiled. His teeth were bright white. It looked weird because the rest of him was so dirty and ragged.

"But I have a feeling he wants to," the old man added quietly.

I shivered. The old man was seriously creeping me out.

POP! A loud noise came from the campfire. We all turned to look.

"What was that?" Cat asked.

Anton was standing by the fire, laughing.

"Anton!" I said. "He threw a firecracker into the fire."

"He's gone!" Egg said suddenly. We all turned. The old man had vanished.

DORKS

The next day, we were really up with the roosters. It was early!

Cat and I managed to get dressed and outside fast. Mr. Spade was standing on the walk outside the bunkhouses.

"Good morning, students," he said. "We're going to start today with a visit to the barn. Follow me!"

Soon we got to the barn. Inside, an old woman was sitting on a stool next to a cow.

"Gather 'round, y'all," the old woman said. "It's time for me to get the milk you kids will need for your breakfast."

"Gross," Anton Gutman said. "I think I'll have waffles instead of cereal!"

For once I had to agree. I prefer my milk from the fridge, not the cow!

"Daisy Mae is just kidding, kids," Deputy Laurie said. I hadn't even seen her come into the barn. "Don't worry. We buy our milk from the store, just like you do," the deputy added.

That was a relief. We watched Daisy Mae milk the cow. It was weird, but kind of cool.

When she was done, Mr. Spade said, "Time for breakfast. Let's head over to the Saloon."

As we left the barn, Egg grabbed my arm.

"Look," Egg said. "There he is."

Egg pointed to the side of the barn. The old man was there. He looked like he was trying to hide.

"We have to talk to him," I said. "I think he knows something about the weird stuff going on."

"And the stolen money?" Gum asked.

"Maybe," I said. "Come on."

The four of us took off running around the side of the barn. But the old man saw us and ran away.

"Wait!"
I called out.
"We want to talk to you."

But when we rounded the corner, the old man had vanished completely.

"Boy, he must know this town pretty well," Gum said. "He always just disappears."

"Yeah," Egg agreed, a little out of breath. "And he's in good shape for an old man."

Suddenly we heard yelling. "Samantha Archer!" said Mr. Spade. "Edward! James! Catalina!"

Oops.

Mr. Spade was angry. He came stomping over to us.

"What do you think you're doing, running off like that?" he said.

"Sorry, Mr. Spade," I said. I was going to say we were trying to find that old man, but it sounded too weird.

"Ha ha," Anton said from behind Mr. Spade. "What a bunch of dorks."

I don't know about Gum, Cat, and Egg, but I sure felt like a dork right then.

DOWN BY THE RIVER

After breakfast, Deputy Laurie rounded up all us students for the first activity of the day.

"I hear there's a prospector's camp down by the stream," she said. She led us down a dusty path.

We could hear the babbling and bubbling of a small stream. Then, as we came over a rise, we spotted a couple of tents near a brook.

"There they are," the deputy said. "Let's go check it out."

We all headed down to the brook. On the shores were three old men. They were using pans and strainers to look for gold in the water.

"Having any luck, boys?" Deputy Laurie asked.

The men didn't say anything, but one of them stood up slowly and turned around. It was the weird old man from town! He winked at me.

"Look!" I said quietly to my friends. "It's him."

Suddenly a loud voice rang out from the town's speaker system: "Deputy Laurie to the office. You have a phone call."

The deputy looked confused. "I'm not expecting any calls," she muttered. "And I can't just leave the class here."

Sheriff Bob walked up. He was holding a leather bag. "You go ahead, Laurie," he said. "I'll stay here with the kids."

Laurie ran off toward the office. "Thanks, Bob," she called back over her shoulder.

The sheriff turned to us. "You kids watch these men work," he said. Then he leaned down and went into one of the prospectors' tents. We all moved closer to the stream.

"What's the pan for?" Gum asked the men. "Are you going to cook some fish?"

One of the old men shook his head. "We're trying to catch something better than fish, son," he said.

"They're looking for gold, Gum," Egg explained.

"That's right," the man said.

"Do you ever find any real gold here?" I asked.

"Okay, kids," the sheriff said suddenly, coming out of the tent. "Activity's over. Let's head back to town."

"We didn't even get to see any gold!" Cat said sadly.

Then I noticed something. "Hey, what happened to the bag you had?" I asked the sheriff.

"What bag?" the sheriff replied.

"You had a leather bag with you when you came down here," Egg said. "I took a photo if you want to see it."

The sheriff laughed. "That's okay, son," he said. Then he added quietly, "That bag wasn't mine. It belonged to one of these men. I was bringing it back for him."

Maybe, I thought, *it was the weird old man's bag. He disappeared right after the sheriff got there!*

THE LAST NIGHT

At the campfire that night, my friends and I sat in a circle.

"If we're going to solve the case of the missing ticket money," Cat said, "we better hurry."

Egg nodded. "Yeah," he said. "We leave in the morning."

"There's Deputy Laurie," I said. "It's time to ask her some questions."

I ran over to the deputy. My friends followed.

"Deputy," I said. "Can I ask you something?"

"Sure," she replied.

"Who called you this morning?" I asked.

The deputy wrinkled her forehead. "That was weird, actually," she replied. "When I got to the office, whoever was on the phone had hung up."

"Hmm," I said. "That is weird."

The deputy walked off.

"Well, that got us nowhere," Egg said.

"Maybe," I replied. "It seems like someone didn't want Deputy Laurie hanging around the prospectors' tents."

I thought for a moment. Then I turned to Egg and said, "Let's take a look at your photos again."

We saw the figure with the big hat again, and the figure with the long hair. One of them showed up in almost every picture, especially when something strange was going on.

"Those two are in all of the pictures," I said.

"Hey, did you guys notice who's missing from all of these pictures?" Gum said.

We thought for a second. Then I got it.

"Your weaselly bunkmate," I said. "Anton!"

Just then, someone leaned over my shoulder to look at the pictures. It was the strange old man.

"That Anton boy is trouble," the old man said, shaking his head. "Just take a look in that bag of tricks he has."

"How do you know about Anton?"
I asked.

"I see things that other folks miss," the old man said.

Suddenly he looked worried. "I better skedaddle," he said. "Here comes Sheriff Bob Ian Grady!" Once again, the old man vanished.

THE BAG OF TRICKS

After lights out, once Eliza was asleep, Cat and I snuck over to Gum and Egg's room. We had to check Anton's bag.

Gum and Egg were still awake. We heard Anton snoring before we even got inside.

Anton's bag was on the floor beside his bed. Gum shined a flashlight so we could see.

Quietly, I pulled the zipper of Anton's bag and stuck my hand in.

My fingers touched something weird. It felt like a head! "Shine the light in here," I whispered. "What is this?"

"Pull it out!" Cat said.

So I did. It wasn't a head at all. Just hair!

Egg whispered, "Why does Anton have a long wig?"

Then I pulled out something else. "Probably the same reason he has this giant hat," I said. "They're disguises."

"Is Anton the person in all the pictures?" Cat asked.

"Looks that way," I said. "He was trying to look like the deputy or the sheriff!"

Then I said louder, "Wake up, Anton, you little rat!"

Anton sat straight up. "Who's there?" he cried out.

"It's just us," I said. "And it's time for you to confess."

"Yeah," Gum said. "You broke the porch, didn't you?"

"And you rigged that can of paint in the Saloon," Cat added.

"And you stole the ticket money!" Egg added.

"Whoa!" Anton replied. "I didn't take the money, I swear!"

"But you did do those other things?" I asked.

"Yes," Anton said. "I set up a couple of pranks. But I would never take money that didn't belong to me."

"That's hard to believe," I said. "Where were you when the money was stolen that first morning?"

"I was at the Saloon setting up the paint can trap," Anton said. "Honest! I don't steal!"

The four of us sat back. "He's telling the truth, I think," Cat said.

I nodded. "Okay," I said. "But why the big hat and the wig?"

Anton shrugged. "They're my normal disguises," he said. "I didn't know the sheriff would have long hair and the deputy would have a big hat."

"Just got lucky?" Gum asked.

"I guess," Anton replied. He yawned. "Can I go back to sleep now?"

The four of us laughed. "Good idea," Egg said. He walked over to his bed and lay down.

Cat and I quietly headed for the door. "I'm pooped anyway," I said.

But we still don't know who stole that money, I thought.

And time was
running out.

B.I.G. FINALE

From the second I fell asleep to the
moment I woke up, my mind kept thinking
about that stolen money.

I dreamed about dollar bills and camp
tickets chasing me down Main Street.
I turned onto First Street to try to get
away, but they were waiting for me at the
blacksmith's. I just couldn't escape.

So when I woke up the next morning, I
was feeling pretty down and tired.

The field trip mystery crew never left a crime unsolved! Never! But it was our last day at Scrub Brush. There was no time left.

It was another hot, dry morning. Gum and Egg walked over to me and Cat as we left our room.

"Can you believe this?" Gum said.

"A crime going unsolved," I said, shaking my head.

"And now the camp will have to close," Cat added.

Feeling bad, the four of us climbed onto the bus. As we walked toward our favorite seats, I saw something on the floor of the bus. I bent over and picked up a wrapper from BIG Burger.

"Who left their trash on the bus?" Cat said.

"That's pretty rude," Gum added.

"I agree," I said. "But it's also the last clue I needed! Come on, guys. I know who took the money!"

"Hey!" Mr. Spade called after us as we ran. "The bus is about to leave!"

But we couldn't stop now. In seconds, we were at the sheriff's office.

I burst through the door.

Sheriff Bob was on the phone. "The camp will have to close," he said into the phone. "With that money gone, the old man's broke." He laughed. "I'm sure he'll be ready to sell to BIG Stop now," he said.

"I knew it!" I said. "Sheriff Bob is none other than Bob Ian Grady. B.I.G.!"

"Big?" Egg said. "Oh! As in BIG Stop!"

The sheriff turned to us. The whole class, Mr. Spade, and Deputy Laurie were behind us at the door.

To my surprise, the sheriff didn't freak out or try to escape. Instead, he laughed.

"Yes," he said. "I am Bob Ian Grady, president of the BIG Stop Restaurant Corporation."

Deputy Laurie looked shocked. "I had no idea," she said.

"You mean that's not why you two were arguing?" I asked.

The deputy shook her head. "I was just mad he got the sheriff part instead of me," she said. "He doesn't even know how to lasso!"

"We thought you were in on it," I said.

Deputy Laurie gasped. "No way," she told me. "I never knew Bob was doing anything wrong."

"That man is a criminal," I said.

Mr. Grady laughed again. Then he said, "I own BIG Stop. But that's no crime."

"But it is a crime to steal the ticket money so the land will have to be sold to you!" I replied.

"You can't prove a thing," Mr. Grady replied. "Anyhow, you kids have a bus to catch. Thank you for visiting Scrub Brush. Now run along!"

The sheriff turned in his chair and pretended to ignore us. He wanted to go back to his phone call.

But just then, one more person came bursting into the sheriff's office.

It was the weird old man.

"We can prove it, Grady," the old man said. "I found this in the prospectors' tent by the brook."

He held up a leather bag. Then he turned it over. Piles of money fell onto the office floor.

"The ticket money!" Deputy Laurie said.

The sheriff shrugged. "So?" he said. "One of those actors who play the prospectors did it. You can't prove I had anything to do with it."

"Oh yes we can," Egg said. "I have a photo of you holding that bag and going into the tent. That's all the proof the real police will need."

"That and probably some fingerprints," I added.

Suddenly Sheriff Bob's face turned pale. He looked at the old man.

"How did you find that bag?" the fake sheriff asked. "No one uses those tents. They're just props! The actors have their own rooms."

"I'm no actor," said the old man. Then he pulled off his ragged hat and overcoat. "I have been sleeping in that tent all weekend, watching over this camp, and keeping this land safe!"

Suddenly I recognized him. "You're the man I saw at the BIG Stop on our way here, aren't you?" I asked. "Arguing with that businesswoman."

The man nodded. "That's right, young lady," he said. "That woman was Grady's assistant."

Egg scratched his chin. "But who are you?" he asked.

"Why, I'm Jeb Brush," the old man said. "I own this camp!"

Mr. Spade stepped forward and shook Mr. Brush's hand. "Good to meet you, Mr. Brush," our teacher said. "Thanks to these crime-solving students, I guess you're going to own this camp a little longer."

Mr. Brush smiled and winked at my friends and me. "This camp will be around a long time," he said. "Thanks to these kids. But no thanks to Bob Ian Grady!"

I looked over at the fake sheriff. He was trying to climb out the window! "Stop him!" I yelled.

All of the kids in my class ran over and grabbed Mr. Grady.

Deputy Laurie put the sheriff in handcuffs. "I'm not a real deputy," she said. "But these are real handcuffs."

"You can't stop me," Mr. Grady said. "I'll own this land somehow!" I thought he looked like he was going to cry.

The deputy pulled the sheriff out of the office. "Explain it to the real cops," she told him.

"All right, class," Mr. Spade said. "Let's head home."

Mr. Spade led the class back to the bus. We all filed on. Cat, Gum, Egg, and I sat in the very back row, like always.

The driver started up the engine and the bus slowly pulled away from the camp.

"Will we stop for a snack again, Mr. Spade?" the driver asked.

Mr. Spade looked at me, Cat, Gum, and Egg.

"Yes, we'll stop for a snack, Willy," he said. "Just anywhere but BIG Stop!"

literary news

MYSTERIOUS WRITER REVEALED!

▶ SAINT PAUL, MN

Steve Brezenoff lives in St. Paul, Minnesota, with his wife, Beth, their son, Sam, and their small, smelly dog, Harry. Besides writing books, he enjoys playing video games, riding his bicycle, and helping middle-school students work on their writing skills. Steve's ideas almost always come to him in his dreams, so he does his best writing in his pajamas.

arts & entertainment

CALIFORNIA ARTIST IS KEY TO SOLVING MYSTERY – POLICE SAY

Early on, C. B. Canga's parents discovered that a piece of paper and some crayons worked wonders in taming the restless dragon. There was no turning back. In 2002 he received his BFA in Illustration from the Academy of Arts University in San Francisco. He works at the Academy of Arts as a drawing instructor. He lives in California with his wife, Robyn, and his three kids.

A Detective's Dictionary

confess (kuhn-FESS)—to admit that you did something

crooks (KRUKS)—people who have committed crimes

deputy (DEP-yoo-tee)—a person whose job is to help a sheriff

evidence (EV-uh-duhnss)—proof that a crime was committed

grub (GRUHB)—food

prospector (PRAH-spek-tur)—someone who looks for gold

rigged (RIGD)—set up

saloon (suh-LOON)—a place to eat and drink

sheriff (SHARE-if)—someone who is in charge of fighting crime

swaggered (SWAG-urd)—walked confidently

urgent (UR-juhnt)—very important

Samantha Archer
Mr. Spade's homeroom
April 15th

(A) Famous Crooks in the Wild West

The American Frontier is famous for many things, like gold prospectors, the Oregon Trail, and covered wagons. But it is also known for criminal activity. Some of the things that happened in the Wild West make Mr. Grady's crimes look like they were no big deal!

One of the most famous Wild West criminals was Jesse James. He and his brother, Frank James, and their James Gang were most famous for robbing banks and trains all over the American West in many different states. Jesse James was killed by someone he thought he could trust, the brother of one of his friends.

Another famous Wild West outlaw was Billy the Kid. Born as Henry McCarty, and also known as William H. Bonney, Billy the Kid was famous for stealing horses.

John Henry "Doc" Holliday, a dentist who became a bartender and a sharpshooter, was known as one of the best gunfighters in the West. He was also known for getting into violent fights.

As you can see, Mr. Grady isn't the worst criminal the Wild West has ever seen. However, none of the other men listed here ever messed with a sixth-grade field trip.

Samantha: Well done. This is a good collection of Wild West crooks. (Did you know that there were female Wild West outlaws too? One of the most famous, Belle Starr, was known as the Female Jesse James!)—Mr. S.

1. In this book, the whole sixth grade (including me) went on a field trip. What field trips have you gone on? Which one was your favorite, and why?

2. Why was Bob Grady trying to get Scrub Brush to close?

3. Egg, Gum, Cat, and I thought that Anton had committed the crimes. Why do you think we thought that?

IN YOUR OWN DETECTIVE'S NOTEBOOK . . .

1. I live in a house with my grandparents. Write about where you live, and who you live with.

2. Gum, Egg, Cat, and I are best friends. Write about your best friend. Don't forget to include what you like about your friend.

3. This book is a mystery story. Write your own mystery story!

THEY SOLVE CRIMES, CATCH CROOKS, CRACK CODES... AND RIDE THE BUS BACK TO SCHOOL AFTERWARD.

Meet Egg, Gum, Sam, and Cat.
Four sixth-grade detectives and best
friends. Wherever field trips take them,
mysteries aren't far behind . . .

FIELD TRIP MYSTERIES

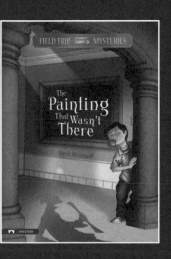

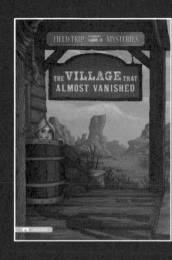

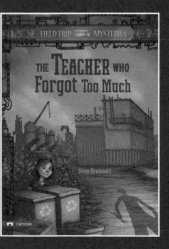

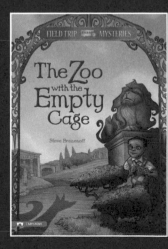

www.stonearchbooks.com